FLO

A CHILD'S GOOD MORNING BOOK

By **Margaret Wise Brown**

Illustrated by **Karen Katz**

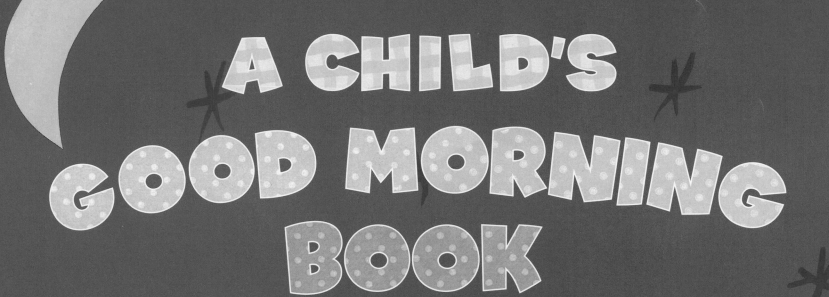

HarperCollins*Publishers*

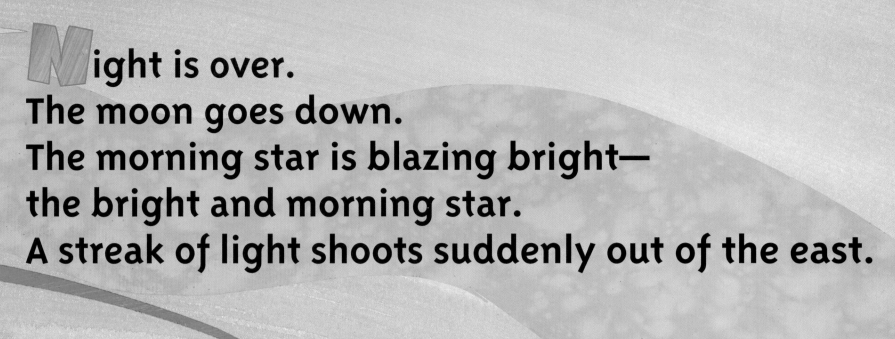

Night is over.
The moon goes down.
The morning star is blazing bright—
the bright and morning star.
A streak of light shoots suddenly out of the east.

Bright golden moment
on the ledges of the sea.

The sun has risen
in the green of a tree.

crow to the dawning day.

The birds in the tree tops begin to chirp and twitter.

Wake up birds

and fly away into the morning, into the day.

The sun rises higher over the edge of the land.

A squirrel pops out of his hole in the tree.

Who woke me up?

The sun!

The sun is up!

It shines on the horses
in the wild fields of morning.

Wake up little horses!
The sun is up.
Gallop away.

Wake up squirrel.
Frisk away.

In the valley beyond the hill
the sheep are still huddled together
in their warm soft blanket of wool.

Wake up, sheep. The sun comes over the hill.

The sun warms the dark valley.
It warms and wakes up the sheep.

It wakes up the goats and the little rabbits that

leap and run and nibble their way through the day.

The flowers open to the morning sun.

The thistles unclose,
the primrose,
the daisies,
and the wild
pink rose.

And the bees begin to buzz.

Wake up, bees,

and buzz through the murmuring day.

The morning glory climbs the vine.

The bugs are creeping.
One bug is still sleeping.

Wake up, bug!

Alarm clocks ring.

Small birds sing.

And in all the clocks the ticks grow softer than the tocks.

The children get up
and put on their socks.

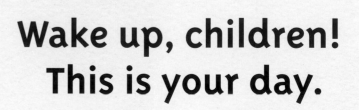

Wake up, children!
This is your day.

What will
you think?

What will
you play?

Wake up,

everyone!

This is your day.

To my basketball girl, Lena.

Special thanks to Martha and Whitney.

—K.K.

A Child's Good Morning Book

Illustrations copyright © 2009 by Karen Katz

Manufactured in China.

For information address HarperCollins Children's Books, a division of HarperCollins Publishers,

1350 Avenue of the Americas, New York, NY 10019.

www.harpercollinschildrens.com

Library of Congress Cataloging-in-Publication Data is available.

ISBN 978-0-06-128864-7 (trade bdg.) — ISBN 978-0-06- 128861-6 (lib. bdg.)

Design by Martha Rago

1 2 3 4 5 6 7 8 9 10

❖

Newly illustrated edition, 2009